DATE DUE	
GAYLORD	PRINTED IN U.S.A.

BIOME BATTLES Book 6

Operation Ocean

by Bob Temple   illustrated by Savannah Horrocks

CC 5195
10.00
JF
8/09

PICTURE WINDOW BOOKS
Minneapolis, Minnesota

Editor: Jill Kalz
Designers: Nathan Gassman and Hilary Wacholz
Page Production: Michelle Biedscheid
Associate Managing Editor: Christianne Jones
The illustrations in this book were created
with watercolor and ink.

Picture Window Books
5115 Excelsior Boulevard
Suite 232
Minneapolis, MN 55416
877-845-8392
www.picturewindowbooks.com

Printed in the United States of America.

Library of Congress Cataloging-in-Publication Data
Temple, Bob.
Operation ocean / by Bob Temple ; illustrated by
Savannah Horrocks.
p. cm. - (Read-it! chapter books: Biome Battles ; 6)
ISBN 978-1-4048-3650-1 (library binding)
[1. Oceans-Fiction. 2. Prophecies-Fiction.
3. Adventure and adventurers-Fiction. 4. Youths'
art.] I. Horrocks, Savannah, 1985 ill. II. Title.
PZ7.T2430p 2008
[Fic]-dc22   2007033075

Table of Contents

Ari

A curious boy who many Imps believe is one of the two humans mentioned in the Imp Prophecy

Kendra

Ari's best friend and co-adventurer who many Imps believe is the other human from the Imp Prophecy

Troll King

Leader of the Trolls, a group of large, mean, smelly creatures who seek to rule the world by destroying the biomes and turning Earth into a wasteland

Tundra

Rain Forest

Desert

MAP and CHARACTER KEY

Trace

Son of King Crag, the Imp King, and Ari and Kendra's guide through the world's biomes

King Crag

Leader of the Imps, a group of small, gentle creatures who protect all of Earth's biomes from harm

Prairie

Wetlands

IMP VILLAGE

Ocean

A Friendship Torn

Ari lay in his bedroom and waited for something—anything—to happen. A strange feeling came over him. Nothing felt right. He felt alone, but at the same time, he felt like he was surrounded.

Sometimes, he just wanted to get away from everything. He wanted to go back to the way things used to be. Other times, the many mysteries in his life made Ari want to keep searching for answers.

It had been six months since the noises first came from his closet. A knock, a click, a whistle. A knock, a click, a whistle.

Finally, one day, a small, dark figure had come to Ari and changed his life forever. It was Trace, the Imp. He had come to take Ari and his friend Kendra to the Imp world.

Ari and Kendra had joined the Imps in their battles against the evil Trolls. The Trolls lived underground. Unable to survive in sunlight, clean air, and water, they sought to destroy the planet's biomes. The Trolls were defeated in the rain forest, the tundra, the wetlands, the desert, and the prairie. Their final battle would be in the ocean.

Along the way, Ari and Kendra learned of the Imp Prophecy. It told of two young humans who would help the Imps and lead them to victory over the Trolls, once and for all. The humans and the Imps would save the world.

It had all sounded so exciting. Though scared from time to time, Ari and Kendra loved their adventures. They learned some amazing things about themselves, too. Ari could breathe underwater. When scared, Kendra could turn into a prairie dog.

They had also learned some strange things. Ari found that he had things in common with the Imp king. He wondered if he was King Crag's son, and Trace's brother. Kendra struggled to figure out her role in these adventures.

But never had the two friends returned with so much unsettled. Kendra had been

pulled through to the Imp world without Ari
for the first time. She had found her ability
to change form. She had also learned that
King Crag had switched sides and joined
the Trolls.

It had been two weeks. Why hadn't Trace come back? With King Crag joining the Trolls, what would become of the Imps?

Worst of all, going to the Imp world alone had caused problems in Kendra's friendship with Ari. They had been best friends for as long as they could remember.

But when Kendra returned from the Imp world, they argued. Ari yelled. Kendra yelled back. Ari said Kendra should not have gone on the prairie adventure alone. Kendra said she'd had no choice.

Neither of them had spoken to each other in two weeks. All Ari could do was wait.

Joining Forces

Ari listened to the clock ticking in his room.

Tick, tock. Tick, tock. Tick, tock.

It was the middle of the night. Ari's room

was pitch black. But Ari couldn't sleep. He just lay there thinking. And thinking. And thinking some more.

Tick, tock. Tick, tock. Tick, tock. Tick, blub, blub, blub.

Ari sat up. What was that noise? That wasn't just the clock. It was different. It sounded like bubbling water.

Ari turned on the light and looked at the floor. He didn't see anything unusual. Everything was dry. Still, the bubbling noise continued. Ari knew what that meant. He knew what he needed to do. He needed to get Kendra right away.

Ari jumped out of bed, threw on some clothes, and ran out the back door. The strange bubbling noise meant that Trace the Imp was coming back—and soon.

For now, any thoughts of troubles with Kendra were gone.

When Ari reached Kendra's backyard, he looked up and saw that her bedroom light was on. Kendra was sitting by the window, looking out into the night.

Ari picked up a small stone and tossed it toward the glass.

Nothing. The stone didn't make a sound.

Then, as Ari reached down for another stone, his first one came back down and hit him on the head.

"The window is open, you dope," Kendra laughed.

"Kendra," Ari said, "you have to come over to my house. I think Trace is coming back."

"Bubbling sounds?" Kendra asked. "Are you hearing bubbling sounds, too?"

"Yeah!" Ari said.

"I'm coming down," Kendra said. "But first, I'm putting on my swimsuit. Something tells me I'll need it."

Salt Air

As he waited for Kendra, Ari practiced his apology. He knew he shouldn't have yelled at Kendra for going on an adventure alone. After all, it wasn't really her choice.

Still, saying he was sorry was never easy, especially when he had to say it to Kendra.

Ari heard the back door open. Kendra tiptoed outside.

"OK," she whispered, "let's go."

"Um, Kendra?" Ari said. He paused for a moment. Kendra stared at him, her hands on her hips.

"What? What? We're wasting time here," she said.

"Kendra," Ari said, "I'm sor—"

"Oh, quit it," Kendra said. "I know, you're sorry. So am I. We don't need some big, mushy moment here, do we? Let's go!"

Ari let out a big breath. Kendra had forgiven him. It felt good to be friends with her again.

In a split second, Kendra was gone. She jumped over hedges and headed toward Ari's house. He ran after her.

When they got to the house, the two
friends crept inside. "This time, we stay
together, right?" Ari said, taking her hand.

Kendra nodded. Up the stairs they went.
They both knew what they wanted to see
in the hallway. And neither of them was
disappointed. They looked down the hallway
just in time to see the small figure disappear
through Ari's bedroom door.

"Trace," they whispered.

The closer Ari and Kendra got to the door, the louder the bubbling sounds became. By the time the kids reached the door, they could smell the sea air on the other side.

"Looks like it's time for a swim," Ari said as he turned the doorknob.

When the door swung open, Ari and Kendra gasped.

Huge waves crashed against sharp rocks along a wide-open beach. Seagulls flapped and squawked overhead. A cool, salty breeze whipped through the kids' hair.

Ari stepped through first. Kendra followed. Before either one of them could say a word, their tiny friend popped out from behind one of the rocks. He waved

them closer. Ari and Kendra wasted little time and ran to him.

"Trace! I've been wondering where you've been!" Ari said. He forgot that Trace could not speak outside the walls of the Imp village. "Has your father changed his mind? Has he come back to the Imps?"

4

More to Tell

Trace lowered his head and shook it from side to side. Despite his sadness, he seemed glad to see Ari and Kendra. He waved for them to follow, and the three headed off toward the Imp village.

It was a long walk, but the excitement of what lay ahead made it seem short. Ari and Kendra stayed behind Trace as they hiked up the side of a hill. When they reached the village wall, Kendra saw they were at the top of a cliff overlooking the ocean.

Trace did as he had done before. He held tightly to Ari and Kendra's hands and walked them quickly through the wall.

On the other side, Ari and Kendra had no time to take in the beauty of the Imp village.

"He is down there," Trace said, pointing over the wall, toward the ocean. "The Trolls took him. He is not coming back."

"What do you mean, he's not coming back?" Ari said. "How do you know?"

"One night, my father came into the village," Trace said. "I did not see him.

I was sleeping. He sneaked into my room and left a note for me."

Ari and Kendra looked at each other. They had gotten a lot of notes in their

adventures. Most of them created more questions than they answered.

"Can we see it?" Kendra asked.

"No!" Trace shouted. He then quickly bowed his head. "I am sorry. It is just that much of what my father said in the note was meant only for me. I am sorry. I cannot share it with you."

Ari raised an eyebrow. "Can you at least tell us the part about him not coming back?" he asked.

Trace paused. It was clear that he was trying to be careful about what he was about to say. His pointy ears twitched a little as he thought.

"My father is trying to answer an old riddle, a mystery," Trace said. "He believes that the answer lies with the Trolls. But he is wrong. He is looking in the wrong place. I know it!"

Now Ari and Kendra were more confused than ever. Ari thought back to the talk he had in his bedroom with King Crag. The king had asked questions about Ari's father. Ari didn't know the answers because he had never known his father.

All of the clues to the Imp Prophecy seemed to point to Ari being the son of King Crag. But when Ari suggested it to the king, the king had said, "Do not be so sure that you understand the past. I, too, have wondered many things. I have many questions. And I know where to get answers." After that, the king had gone to join the Trolls.

Why would the Trolls know anything about Ari's past?

"What is he looking for?" Ari asked.

"He is looking for answers to the mystery of the prophecy," Trace said. "But he will

not find them with the Trolls. He will find
only trouble. The Trolls plan to pollute
the ocean water. The entire planet will be
doomed if they destroy the oceans, Ari.

Without my father's leadership, I do not
know how the Imps
can stop the Trolls."

"But your father
doesn't believe the
Imp Prophecy,"
Kendra said. "He
doesn't believe
we are the two
humans who are
supposed to help
the Imps defeat
the Trolls. Right?"

Trace paused
again. He
crouched down
to the ground and
scratched in the dirt with a stick.
He was growing nervous.

"You see," he said, looking back up at

Ari and Kendra, "he does not *think* you could be the two humans from the prophecy. But I *know* you are. I *know* it is true."

"How do you know it's true?" Ari asked, stepping toward Trace. "What are you keeping from us?"

Trace shuddered. "I cannot tell you," he said. "Not yet. Soon. It is just—"

"What is it?" Kendra asked.

"There is more to the Imp Prophecy than I have ever told you," Trace said. "There is much more!"

Then Trace disappeared.

Finding the King

"Look! There!" Kendra said. She pointed at a tiny mouse running away. "That's him!"

"That's who?" Ari asked.

"Trace!" Kendra yelled. "He got scared and turned into a mouse!"

Ari remembered Kendra telling the story of how she had turned into a prairie dog when the Trolls had scared her. Changing form let her run to safety and dig out of the Trolls' underground tunnels.

"Is that what happened to you?" Ari asked, his eyes wide.

"Pretty much," Kendra said. "Maybe I'm part Imp, too."

They both laughed, then realized that maybe it wasn't so funny. Now they were stuck inside the Imp village. They were unable to get out without Trace's help.

"We have to get to the ocean to find King Crag and stop the Trolls for good," Ari said.

"Maybe it isn't just Trace," Kendra said. "Maybe any Imp can help us get through the village wall. Let's go find someone."

Ari and Kendra headed toward the center of the Imp village. It was as beautiful as ever. Kendra's favorite part—the tall, thin waterfall that seemed to come from the sky—fell gently into a beautiful lake. The king's house sat alone in the center of the village, as always.

But this time, there was something different. It was very, very quiet. The happy sounds of Imps playing, singing, and working were gone. In fact, there wasn't an Imp to be seen. Ari and Kendra were all alone. All of the Imps in the village were gone.

Now, Ari and Kendra *really* didn't know how they were going to get out of the village.

As night fell, the silence became eerie. It was *too*

quiet. Ari and Kendra thought they saw something moving near the wall. Soon, the ground shook with the heavy footsteps of giant creatures.

Ari and Kendra tried to run, but it was too late. The creatures were coming at them too fast.

"Trolls!" Ari yelled.

6

Captured

The Trolls picked up Ari and Kendra in their huge hands. Each Troll held one of the kids in front of his drippy, drooling face.

"We've got them!" the Trolls cried.

Soon dozens of Trolls gathered around. Their nasty faces, together with their large size and bad smell, made them very scary. But Kendra was not scared enough to change form.

"Take them to the ocean!" another Troll shouted. "Lock them away until we know the truth!"

The Trolls carrying Ari and Kendra led the way toward the village wall. There, King Crag waited for them.

"So that's how the Trolls got into the Imp village," Ari said. "You! We all trusted you! You tricked us!"

King Crag didn't blink. He held each Troll's hand and, two by two, led them back out of the Imp village. He didn't speak or look at Ari and Kendra. It was clear that he no longer cared about them.

King Crag still looked like an Imp, but he had become a Troll.

The Trolls climbed down the steep walls of the cliff. When they reached the shore, they dug through the sandy beach and opened a hole into their tunnel system.

Once underground, the Trolls locked Ari and Kendra in a cage beneath the ocean floor. A few feet above them, colorful fish swam, dolphins played, and large sea turtles glided through the water. Kendra wished she could see it all.

"Stand guard," one of the Troll guards said to the other.

"They can't get out," the other Troll said.

"Why do we need to guard them?"

"We must make sure those two stay Trolls," the first one said. "We can't let the mistake of 12 years ago repeat itself."

The Trolls nodded at each other. They took a few steps away and talked quietly. Ari and Kendra struggled to hear more.

"What was *that* all about?" Kendra asked. "What did he mean by 'stay Trolls'?"

"I have no clue," Ari said. "What do you think happened 12 years ago?"

"How should I know?" Kendra said. "We were babies 12 years ago."

Just then, they heard a familiar voice outside the cage. It quickly quieted the talking guards.

"You may go," the voice said to the guards. "They will not escape. We all know where they belong now. I will stay here with them."

The guards nodded and walked away. King Crag stood at the edge of the cage.

Ari and Kendra didn't look at him. Now that he was helping the Trolls, they wanted

nothing to do with him.

Once the Troll guards turned a corner and were out of sight, King Crag leaned against the cage bars and spoke.

"Children, listen to me," the king said.

Ari and Kendra ignored him.

"Children, please listen," the king said again, trying to keep his voice down.

Ari and Kendra heard, but they didn't look at him.

"Children," the king said, "you do not understand. It is not what you think. You must help me get out of here!"

Rising Tide

Now Ari and Kendra turned around.

"Wait a minute," Ari said. "We thought you were a Troll. Which side are you on?"

"You do not understand," the king said.

"I am the Imp king. I have always been the Imp king."

Kendra spoke up. "We're not helping you do anything until we get some answers to some questions."

There was silence. Ari and Kendra looked at each other. Deep down, they both wanted to help the king. But he needed to earn their trust first.

"We can escape," the king said. "It is still night. Most of the Trolls are above ground. The tide is out, so there is little water above you. If we dig for the surface now, we can get away."

Ari and Kendra jumped up on their chairs. They began to dig at the ceiling above them.

"Thanks for the tip," Ari said, digging fast. "Kendra and I are getting out. You, I'm afraid, are on your own."

"Listen!" the king shouted. Both of the kids stopped and turned to the king. "I will explain it all, but we have to go quickly. The tide will be coming back in soon."

"Fine," Kendra said. "Tell us what's going on."

The king took a deep breath. "Things have not always been as they are today," he began. "Trolls and Imps have not always been at war. There was a time when Trolls and Imps lived together peacefully."

Ari and Kendra were interested now. They stopped digging.

"The Troll king and I had an understanding," King Crag said. "Imps would rule the surface of Earth, and Trolls would rule the underground. Then, one day, everything changed."

"What changed it?" Ari asked.

"Two babies were found on the shore of

the ocean," the king said. "Human babies."

"Us?" Kendra asked.

King Crag ignored the question.

"Well, we *thought* they were human," he said. "But there was something different about them. The Imps thought the babies were very Imp-like. Many thought the babies were sent to lead us, or to protect us.

"The Trolls felt the same way. They thought the babies were very Troll-like. Both sides knew that whoever ended up with the babies would have great power, for these were special babies.

"There were many fights. These fights grew into battles. It seemed as though our world was about to break apart. And then, one day—"

The king struggled for the words.

"One day, the babies were gone. Gone forever," he said. "The Imps believed the Trolls were hiding them, training them to be Trolls. The Trolls thought we Imps were hiding them. This is how the Imp Prophecy began. The Imps believed that one day, these special children would return, to help us defeat the Trolls."

Ari and Kendra were speechless.

"After I first saw you two, I wondered," the king said. "But I still thought the Trolls were hiding these children. I tricked them into thinking that I was joining them, so I could find out the truth."

"So?" Ari said. "What did you find out?"

The Truth

Seawater dripped from the ceiling. The tide was coming back in. With each wave, more water spilled into the cage. In just a few minutes, tons of water poured in.

Ari and Kendra tried to widen the hole to escape. King Crag quickly unlocked the cage and tried to help. Water pooled around their feet.

Suddenly, the cage door slammed shut. Standing there was the Troll king.

"I heard every word!" he bellowed. "Whatever you think you've learned here,

Crag, don't be so sure! I have known all along what you were trying to do. Now you will drown with these two fakes!"

With the clean ocean water burning his feet, the Troll king wrapped a heavy chain around the cage door. He locked it and ran. The salty seawater was already up to Ari and Kendra's waists.

Just then, Ari remembered his special skill. "Wait a minute!" he said. "I can breathe underwater!"

"That's great for you," Kendra said. "But I don't know how that's going to help the king and me."

Ari's heart sank. The water was now up to his shoulders. King Crag was clinging to his neck. Ari and Kendra got back up on their chairs. They knew only a few short minutes were left.

With each inch of rising water, the last bits of hope faded.

"Kendra," Ari said as the water reached their shoulders again. "Once the water fills the room, it won't rush in anymore. I'll try to dig the hole out wider and pull you and the king through."

"No way," Kendra said. "You have to get out of here. If we *are* the humans from the

Imp Prophecy, you have to escape and help Trace lead the Imps." She smiled weakly. "At least it feels good to know that all of the Trolls will drown down here, too."

The water rose to Kendra's chin. She got scared. The king got scared too as the water met his nose.

"Stay calm!" Ari yelled. "It'll be OK. I'll get you out!"

Kendra and the king feared they were dying. It looked hopeless. As the water finally reached the ceiling, Ari felt the king let go of his hand. Ari swam straight for the hole to try to widen it. When he got there, he saw two tiny, brightly colored fish swim out through the small opening.

Ari looked around the cage below for Kendra and King Crag. It was empty. Ari realized what had happened. He dug at the edges of the hole and widened it so he could squeeze through.

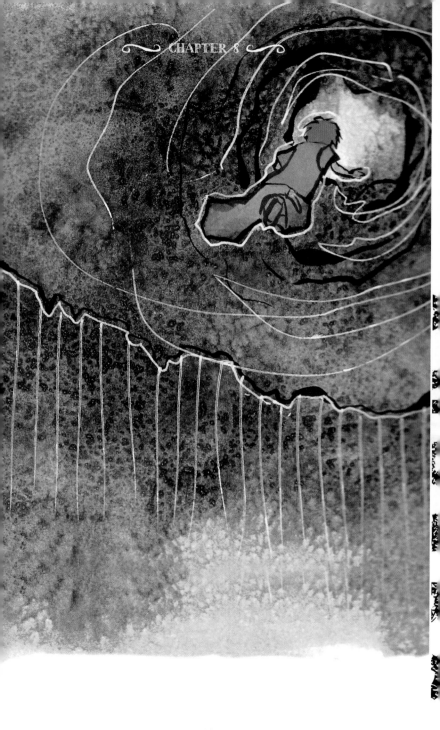

Ari swam hard for the shore. He found Kendra and the king standing on the sand next to Trace.

"Seems I have something in common with the king, too," Kendra said, smiling. "Sometimes, a little fear goes a long way."

"First you turn into a prairie dog, and now a fish. I can't wait to see what you turn into next," Ari said.

The king gave the kids a hug to say thank you, then headed back to the village. Trace, unable to speak outside the village walls, took Ari and Kendra's hands and led them back to the edge of the Imp world.

It was a long, slow journey. Each of them knew that it was probably their last walk together.

Before they knew it, Trace had pulled them through Ari's bedroom door and into the hallway outside it. He smiled at them, winked, and disappeared.

Just as he had done many times before, Ari opened his hand to find a crumpled piece of paper, put there by Trace. He flattened it out, smiled at Kendra, and read these words aloud:

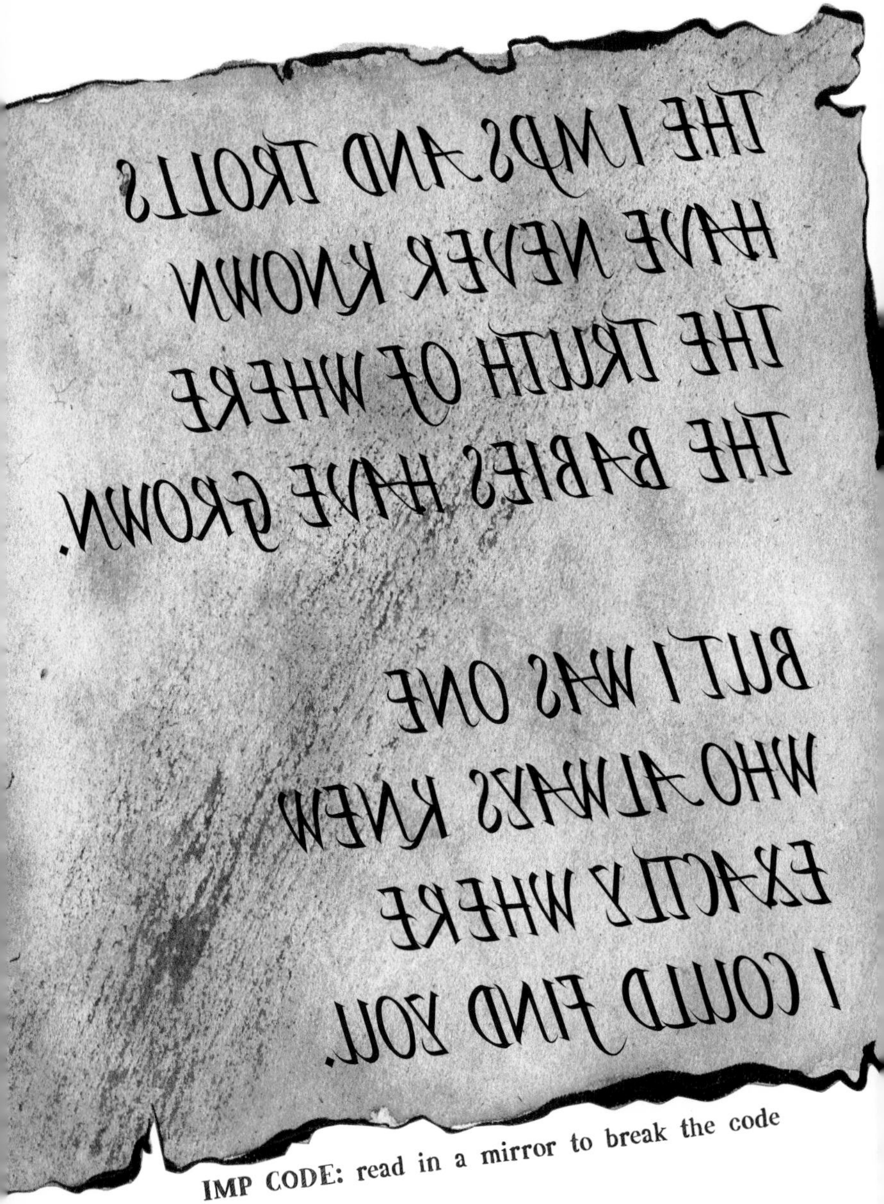

THE IMPS AND TROLLS
HAVE NEVER KNOWN
THE TRUTH OF WHERE
THE BABIES HAVE GROWN.

BUT I WAS ONE
WHO ALWAYS KNEW
EXACTLY WHERE
I COULD FIND YOU.

IMP CODE: read in a mirror to break the code

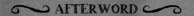

AFTERWORD

What Is an Ocean?

Oceans are very large bodies of saltwater. They cover more than 70 percent of Earth's surface and contain nearly 97 percent of all of the water in the world. There are five oceans: the Pacific Ocean, the Atlantic Ocean, the Indian Ocean, the Arctic Ocean, and the Southern Ocean.

Ocean Plants and Animals

The oceans are home to billions of plants and animals. The most common plant is called phytoplankton. These are very tiny plants that float near the surface of the water. Other ocean plants include kelp and seagrass.

Thousands of species of fish live in the oceans. So do reptiles such as sea turtles and sea snakes. Seabirds such as penguins, gulls, and pelicans spend some time in the water and some time out of the water. Even mammals such as dolphins, whales, and sea otters live in the oceans.

The largest group of ocean animals are invertebrates, which have no backbone. Jellyfish, lobsters, sponges, and coral are all examples of invertebrates.

Why Are Oceans Important?

People, plants, and animals need water to survive. Oceans supply the world with water through the water cycle. When the sun heats the ocean, water on the ocean's surface changes into a gas. The gas floats up into the air and forms droplets. Those droplets later fall to the ground as rain or snow. Rivers carry the water back to the ocean, and the water cycle begins again.

Oceans also help to keep the planet's average temperature from getting too hot or too cold. They absorb the sun's rays. The heat energy is then carried around the globe by ocean waves and currents. Oceans heat up the land and air in the winter and cool them off during the summer.

Operation Ocean

ON THE WEB

FactHound offers a safe, fun way to find Web sites related to topics in this book. All of the sites on FactHound have been researched by our staff.

1. Visit *www.facthound.com*
2. Type in this special code: 1404836500
3. Click on the FETCH IT button.

Your trusty FactHound will fetch the best sites for you!

LOOK FOR ALL OF THE BOOKS
IN THE SCIENCE TALES SERIES:
Rescuing the Rain Forest (Book 1)
Taking Back the Tundra (Book 2)
War Over the Wetlands (Book 3)
Danger in the Desert (Book 4)
Protecting the Prairie (Book 5)
Operation Ocean (Book 6)